DOR
and the Goblin

written and illustrated by,
PATRICIA COOMBS

PUFFIN BOOKS

Puffin Books, Penguin Books Ltd, Harmondsworth, Middlesex, England
Penguin Books, 625 Madison Avenue, New York, New York 10022, U.S.A.
Penguin Books Australia Ltd, Ringwood, Victoria, Australia
Penguin Books Canada Ltd, 2801 John Street, Markham, Ontario, Canada L3R 1B4
Penguin Books (N.Z.) Ltd, 182-190 Wairau Road, Auckland 10, New Zealand

First published in Great Britain by World's Work Ltd 1974
Published in Puffin Books 1982

Printed by: Litografía A. Romero, S. A.
Canary Islands (Spain) D. L. TF.: 932 – 1981

For the Fern Place School Library

This is Dorrie. She is a witch. A little witch. Her socks never match. Sometimes her shoes are on the wrong feet. Sometimes her hat is inside out. She lives with her black cat, Gink, and her mother, the Big Witch, and Cook.

One day Dorrie went downstairs with a pack of cards. Gink went with her.

The Big Witch was rushing around the parlour. She was getting things out and putting things away. She looked out of the window and frowned. She put a box of candles on the piano and looked out of the window again.

"Mother," said Dorrie. "I still can't do that card trick right. Please show me once more, so I can be in your Magic Show tonight."

"There isn't time!" cried the Big Witch. "I have a hundred things to do. The Short High Sorcerer was going to get a rabbit for the Magic Show and come round to help. He still isn't here. Dorrie, get the laundry basket and bring it inside. I have to iron all the napkins for the Tea. Cook is too busy baking to do it."

Dorrie sighed and put the cards back in her pocket. She went into the kitchen and Gink went with her. Water was boiling, cakes were baking, Cook was muttering. Dorrie opened the back door.

The basket was right in front of the door. The napkins were in it, and so was something else. It moved.

"Mother! Cook!" called Dorrie. "Somebody has left us a surprise."

The Big Witch and Cook came running. They looked at the basket.

"Perhaps it's a baby witch," said Dorrie. "I'd like that."

"Oh, no!" cried the Big Witch, starting to faint.

Dorrie took the basket inside. From under a corner of the wrinkled-up napkins a small furry face with red eyes peered out. A small furry hand reached out and pinched Cook.

"A GOBLIN!" screeched Cook. "Get that creature out of my kitchen! The milk will sour! The cakes will sink! The biscuits will burn!" Cook grabbed a frying pan and swung it at the Goblin.

"Don't hit it!" said Dorrie. "It's just a little one."

"A little Goblin is BIG TROUBLE!" said Cook.

The Big Witch groaned and sat up. "My wonderful Tea and Magic Show will be ruined! The only Goblin spell I know takes a whole WEEK to work. It's too late to cancel the Tea and Magic Show. The Short High Sorcerer is the only one who can get rid of it, and he isn't here yet! Oh dear, oh dear!"

Dorrie picked up the Goblin and tucked it under her arm. "Don't worry, Mother. I'll just take care of it until the Sorcerer gets here. You won't even know it's around."

The Big Witch frowned. The Goblin stuck out its tongue. "Well, all right!" said the Big Witch. "But be careful. And DON'T let it out of your room! Goblins can wreck a house in two minutes."

Up, up, up the stairs went Dorrie with the Goblin under her arm. Gink went with her.

Dorrie put the Goblin on her bed. He looked around with his bright-red eyes. He wriggled his ears. Dorrie laughed. He made a face. Dorrie made a face. He jumped to his feet and hopped up and down. Dorrie hopped up and down. Suddenly the Goblin sprang into the air. He landed on Dorrie's dressing table. In a flash he threw her brush and comb and marbles and clock on the floor. With a squeak, he pulled out all the drawers and jumped from one to the other, tossing clothes into the air and all over the floor.

Before Dorrie could grab him, he draped himself in her socks and began dancing up and down. He stuck out his tongue and screeched happily.

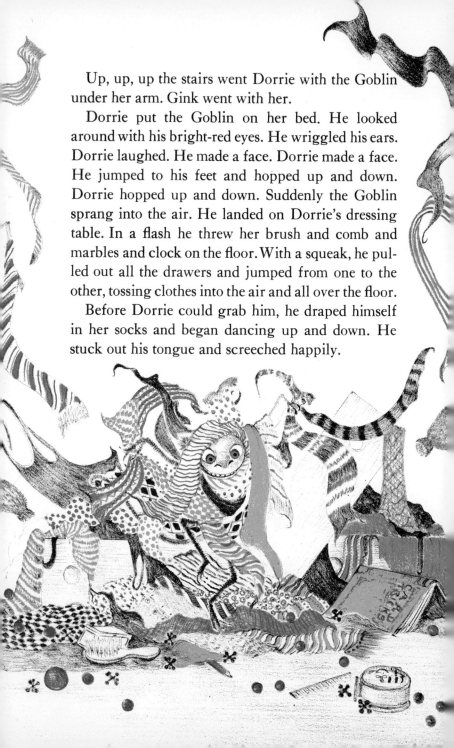

"Oh, my," said Dorrie. "Well, if you like dressing up, I've got a box of old baby clothes in the back of my wardrobe."

Dorrie got the box out. "Come here, Goblin, and stand still."

The Goblin bounded over, rubbing his hands and grinning.

Dorrie put a little black dress on him. And then a striped nightcap on his head.

The Goblin danced up into the air and down. Gink hissed. The Goblin screeched and pinched Gink's tail.

"Don't pinch!" cried Dorrie. "That's cruel!"

The Goblin put his face in his hands, rolled himself into a ball, and rolled under the bed. He kicked the bedsprings so hard one end of the bed fell down with a crash.

"Oh my goodness!" said Dorrie. "Goblin-sitting is hard work." She got her big rubber ball. "Here," said Dorrie. "We'll toss the ball back and forth for awhile. That's quiet."

Dorrie tossed the ball to the Goblin. The Goblin
threw it up into the air, leaped on top of it, and
bounced up and down all around the room. Books
fell out of the bookcase; a chair fell over. He jumped
off the ball, grabbed it in his toes, and threw it right
through the window.

"NO!" cried Dorrie.

Dorrie reached out to grab him. He stuck out his tongue and sailed over her head, snatching her hat. He hung it on top of her cupboard door.

Dorrie climbed up on a chair to get her hat. There was a crash, a thud, and a slam. Dorrie looked round. The Goblin was gone.

Dorrie raced into the hall, and Gink went with her. The Goblin was sliding down the banister. He vanished into the parlour. Dorrie and Gink ran down the stairs and into the parlour after him.

Dorrie looked round. No Goblin. Then she heard a munching sound. She looked behind the curtains. There was the Goblin with the Big Witch's box of candles. He was chewing them up like bananas.

Dorrie dragged him out from behind the curtains. He screeched and screamed and kicked and howled.

Cook came running in. "He just ate a few candles, Cook," said Dorrie. "I think he's hungry."

"BOTHERATION!" cried Cook. "I'd like to stuff him in the washing machine. I'd wash the screeches out of him and iron him flatter than a shadow!"

Dorrie tucked the Goblin under her arm. "I won't let him get out again, Cook," said Dorrie. The Goblin stuck his tongue out at Cook and made faces.

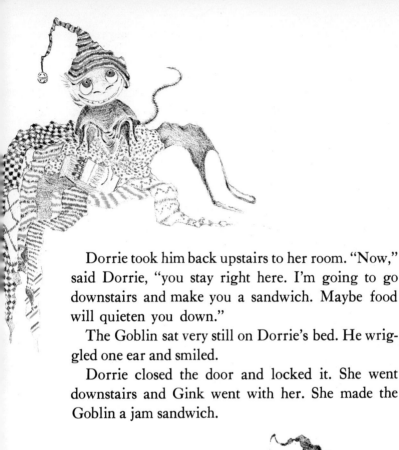

Dorrie took him back upstairs to her room. "Now," said Dorrie, "you stay right here. I'm going to go downstairs and make you a sandwich. Maybe food will quieten you down."

The Goblin sat very still on Dorrie's bed. He wriggled one ear and smiled.

Dorrie closed the door and locked it. She went downstairs and Gink went with her. She made the Goblin a jam sandwich.

Up, up, up the stairs she went and Gink went with her.

Dorrie unlocked her door and opened it. "Goblin, here's a nice. . . ."

Dorrie stopped. The Goblin had her crayons. He was swinging to and fro on her cupboard door, scribbling with the crayons, all over her ceiling.

"OH, NO!" cried Dorrie. "Cook was right. You are BIG TROUBLE. Mother's going to be *so* mad. I wish the Short High Sorcercer were here RIGHT NOW!"

The Goblin winked, grinned wickedly, and sniggered. Reaching out with his tail, he snatched the jam sandwich and stuck it to the ceiling. He clapped and screeched. He leaped into a pile of socks and began tying knots in them.

Dorrie heard the Big Witch calling her. She opened the door.

"Dorrie! Keep that creature QUIET!" said the Big Witch. "I have to practise my Magic Trick before the guests come. You get your clothes changed. The minute the Short High Sorcerer comes, he'll turn that awful Goblin into a black raincloud." The Big Witch slammed her door.

Dorrie looked at the Goblin. "You hear that, Goblin?"

The Goblin put his head down between his hands as if he were going to cry.

He looked so small and so sad Dorrie patted him on his head. "Poor Goblin, don't cry," said Dorrie. "I'll show you my card trick before you get turned into a raincloud, okay?"

The Goblin looked up, grinning. Dorrie took the cards out of her pocket. She began the card trick. A small furry hand slid over and grabbed a card. And another. And another. The Goblin stuffed them into his mouth and began to chew.

"Stop that! You're eating my card trick!" cried Dorrie. "And I was trying to cheer you up. I hope you get a stomachache. I'm going to get dressed for Tea."

Dorrie got a clean dress from the wardrobe, her best shoes, and another pair of socks. She changed her dress and brushed her hair and put her hat on right-side out. She sat down to change her socks. The room was very quiet. She looked round. The Goblin had gone.

"I'm tired of taking care of that stupid Goblin," muttered Dorrie. "I'm going to finish getting dressed and *then* I'll chase him. Maybe Cook will catch him. It would serve him right."

Dorrie took off one shoe. Lightning flashed through the room. She pulled off her sock. Thunder began to rumble. She looked out of the window. The sky was clear. "That's funny," said Dorrie. She started to pull off the other sock, and lightning flashed. She pulled it back on, and the lightning stopped. She put on a shoe. The thunder stopped. She took it off. Thunder began again. A few bubbles floated in through the broken window.

"OH NO!" yelled Dorrie.

Out of her room she went, and Gink went with her. Down the hall they raced, to the little door that led up to the Big Witch's secret room in the tower. The little door was wide open. Up, up, up into the tower went Dorrie and Gink, and into the secret room.

There was the Goblin, sitting in the Big Witch's cauldron. He was blowing bubbles of magic into the air and screeching to himself. Bottles of magic were spilled and splashed all over the room. The cauldron was growing brighter and changing colours.

The Goblin peered over the edge, waving and grinning. His red eyes gleamed through the bubbles.

Dorrie frowned and stamped her foot. "Now you've really got us into terrible trouble," said Dorrie. "Listen to that!"

The Goblin wriggled his ears. From downstairs came booms of thunder and the yells and screams of Cook and the Big Witch.

"You've mixed thunder and lightning into everything in the house, haven't you!"

The Goblin grinned happily and pointed to her hat. Dorrie took it off. A flash of lightning shot across the room. Gink's fur stood on end.

Dorrie jammed her hat back on and grabbed the Goblin. She pushed him into the Big Witch's cupboard and rolled the crystal ball in front of him.

The Goblin put his arms round it and began to lick it like a lollypop.

"Now," muttered Dorrie, "I've got to try to undo this mess you've made."

Dorrie opened the *Big Book of Magic*. The pages were all soggy and stuck together from the spilled magic. Dorrie looked through the recipes. At last she found one under GLUE, GLUP, GOBLIN.

Dorrie began to pour what was left in the bottles of magic into the cauldron: a little bit of blue, a splash of purple, a dash of green, a half bottle of yellow, and a full bottle of red. The Goblin's teeth-marks were in the cork but he hadn't got it open. She sprinkled in some white crystals and a pinch of black.

Dorrie began to stir. Off in the distance there was the whistle of broomsticks as the Wizards and Witches came flying towards the house.

"I've got to *hurry*, Gink, or the Tea and Magic Show will be as big a mess as my room." She spun round to the left and then to the right. She closed her eyes and chanted:

Abacadabra fiddledee doo
Hocus this pocus ten times two
Goblin magic mess undo—
Bubble and simmer
Higgle this piggle
Backward to blue.

Dorrie spun round once more and opened her eyes. Big swirls of coloured smoke rose from the cauldron. Sparks spun through cobwebs and round Dorrie's hat.

There was a faraway BOOM! Then it was still. Even the Big Witch and Cook had stopped shouting downstairs. Outside the window, the Wizards and Witches were stopped motionless in midair.

There was another BOOM! A shower of bright sparks shot out of the cauldron and faded away. Downstairs a clock struck. The Witches and Wizards whizzed into the yard.

Dorrie blinked. A huge Goblin shadow loomed above the cauldron. As it melted into the air, there stood the Short High Sorcerer with a lollypop stuck in his beard. The lollypop was all that was left of the Big Witch's crystal ball.

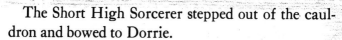

The Short High Sorcerer stepped out of the cauldron and bowed to Dorrie.

"At your service," he said. "You just rescued me from the Goblin spell of an angry Witch. And in the nick of time, too." He took the lollypop from his beard and looked at it. "A few more licks on this crystal ball and I would have been a Goblin for ever. I grant thee a boon."

"Oh my," said Dorrie. "I've had all the booms I need. Thank you just the same."

"*Boon!*" said the Sorcerer, "Not *Boom*. I mean a wish. Any wish within my power."

"Well," said Dorrie. "How about a really good magic card trick? I was so busy taking care of that Goblin I didn't have time to practise."

"A magic card trick! Of course!" said the Short High Sorcerer. He clapped his hands three times and tapped himself on the head with his wand. Then he tapped Dorrie's head and next the pack of cards.

A bell rang downstairs.
"Tea time!" said Dorrie.
And down, down, down
the stairs they went,
Dorrie and Gink and the
Short High Sorcerer.

All the Witches and Wizards were in the parlour. Some of them were frowning at the teapot. Some of them were staring at the napkins. Some of them were hiding behind chairs.

When the Big Witch saw the Sorcerer she jumped up. "At last! You must save us from the Goblin and undo his spell. The napkins have lightning in them, and there is thunder in the teapot!"

The Short High Sorcerer tugged at his beard. "A Goblin problem? A short Goblin with red eyes?"

The Big Witch nodded.

"Dorrie," said the Short High Sorcerer, "snap your fingers and whistle."

Dorrie snapped her fingers and whistled.

"There!" said the Short High Sorcerer. "Now, everyone, unfold your napkins and pour the tea. Dorrie has made the Goblin disappear."

They all had tea and ice-cream and cakes and biscuits. The Short High Sorcerer told them how he had been chasing a rabbit to use in the Magic Show and strayed into the garden of a very cross Witch. She cast a Goblin spell on him so quickly he could not ward it off.

After Tea, everyone did a magic trick. The Big Witch turned her feather duster into a bird, the bird into a hat, and the hat into a feather duster.

Dinger turned his alarm clock into a boot, and out of the boot came dozens of balloons.

Mr. Obs played his violin standing on his head.
Squig juggled six umbrellas at once.

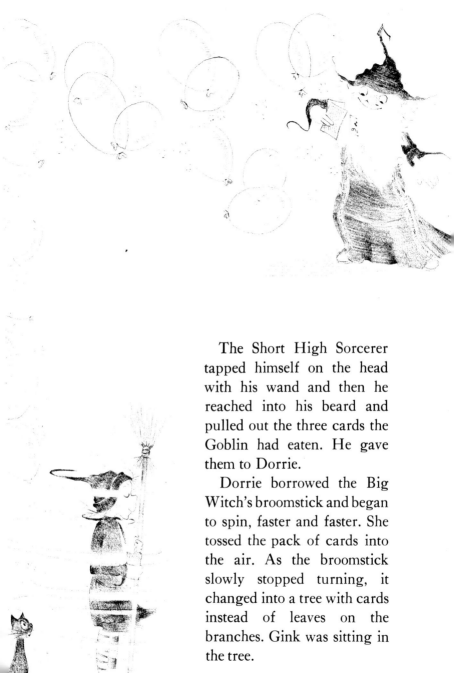

The Short High Sorcerer
tapped himself on the head
with his wand and then he
reached into his beard and
pulled out the three cards the
Goblin had eaten. He gave
them to Dorrie.

Dorrie borrowed the Big
Witch's broomstick and began
to spin, faster and faster. She
tossed the pack of cards into
the air. As the broomstick
slowly stopped turning, it
changed into a tree with cards
instead of leaves on the
branches. Gink was sitting in
the tree.

It was the very best
magic trick of all, and everybody laughed and clapped.

The clock in the hall chimed. The Tea and Magic Show were over.

The Short High Sorcerer was the last to leave. He handed the Big Witch what was left of the lollypop. "Put this in your cauldron overnight with a jam sandwich and three cards. By morning you'll have a new crystal ball."

"Hmmm," said the Big Witch, looking at the lollypop. "I didn't know anything had happened to my old crystal ball. Thank you."

The Short High Sorcerer bowed to Dorrie. Then he gave her his wand. "You'll need this," he whispered, "to mend the bed and the window, and to get the crayon and jam off the ceiling."

Dorrie smiled. "Thank you for the magic card trick. I'll miss you. Come back soon."

The Short High Sorcerer smiled, waved, and floated away into the moonlight with a bunch of balloons.

"I'm glad I didn't hit him with a frying pan when he was a Goblin," said Cook.

"I'm glad the Tea and Magic Show turned out so well," said the Big Witch.

Dorrie yawned. So did Gink. "I'm glad it's bed-time," she said. "Goblin-sitting is hard work."

The End.